**Dear Parents and Caregivers,**

If your child is ready to learn how to read, then you've come to the right place! We want kids to reach for the stars as they begin their reading adventure. With Ready-to-Go!, this very first level has been carefully mapped out to launch their reading voyage.

All books in this level share the following:

★ **Just the right length: each story has about 100 words, many of them repeated.**

★ **Sight words: frequently used words that children will come to recognize by sight, such as "the" and "can."**

★ **Word families: rhyming words used throughout the story for ease of recognition.**

★ **A guide at the beginning that prompts children to sound out the words before they start reading.**

★ **Questions at the end for children to re-engage with the story.**

★ **Fun stories starring children's favorite characters so learning to read is a blast.**

These books will provide children with confidence in their reading abilities as they go from mastering the letters of the alphabet to understanding how those letters create words, sentences, and stories.

***Blast off on this starry adventure . . . a universe of reading awaits!***

# ERIC CARLE

# Can a Cat Do That?

Ready-to-Read

Simon Spotlight
New York   London   Toronto   Sydney   New Delhi

Here is a list of all the words you will find in this book. You might like to sound them out before you begin reading the story.

**Names:**

Butterflies

Horse

Donkey

Rooster

**SIMON SPOTLIGHT**

An imprint of Simon & Schuster Children's Publishing Division · 1230 Avenue of the Americas, New York, New York 10020. This Simon Spotlight edition August 2018. Copyright © 2018 Eric Carle Corporation. Eric Carle's name and signature logo type are registered trademarks of Eric Carle. All rights reserved, including the right of reproduction in whole or in part in any form. SIMON SPOTLIGHT, READY-TO-READ, and colophon are registered trademarks of Simon & Schuster, Inc. For information about special discounts for bulk purchases, please contact Simon & Schuster Special Sales at 1-866-506-1949 or business@simonandschuster.com. Manufactured in the United States of America 1018 LAK 10 9 8 7 6 5 4 3 2 · Library of Congress Cataloging-in-Publication Data Names: Carle, Eric, author, illustrator. Title: Can a cat do that? / Eric Carle. Description: Simon Spotlight edition. | New York : Simon Spotlight, 2018. | Series: The world of Eric Carle | Series: Ready-to-read | Summary: Shows different animals behaving as they normally do, such as running, and asks if a cat can do the same. Includes word list and follow-up questions. Identifiers: LCCN 2017054280 | ISBN 9781534427242 (paperback) | ISBN 9781534427259 (hardcover) Subjects: LCSH: Cats—Habits and behavior—Juvenile fiction. | Animals—Habits and behavior—Juvenile fiction. | CYAC: Cats—Habits and behavior—Fiction. Animals—Habits and behavior—Fiction. | Questions and answers. Classification: LCC PZ10.3.C1896 Can 2018 | DDC [E]—dc23 LC record available at https://lccn.loc.gov/2017054280

## Word families:

| "-at" | → | cat | that |
|-------|---|-----|------|
| "-an" | → | man | can |

## Sight words:

| a | run | do | fly | girl |
|------|-----|-----|-----|------|
| I | me | my | no | read |
| what | yes | | | |

## Bonus words:

| climb | crow | drink | love | loves |
|-------|------|-------|------|-------|
| meow | | | | |

Ready to go? Happy reading!

You might like to try answering the questions about
the story on the last page of this book.

# What can a cat do?

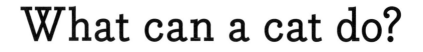

# A horse can run.

# Can a cat do that?

Yes!

# A cat can run.

# A rooster can crow.

# Can a cat do that?

No!

Meow.

# A donkey can drink.

# Can a cat do that?

Yes!

A cat can drink.

# Butterflies can fly.

# Can a cat do that?

No!

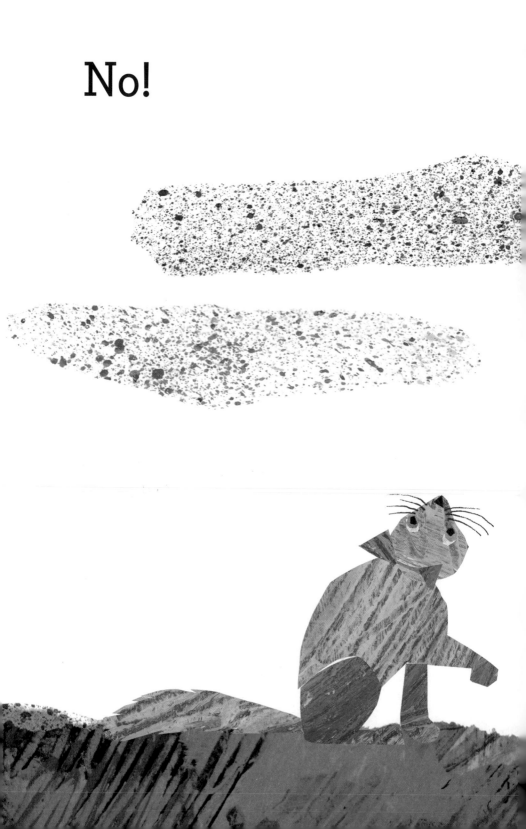

*Meow.*

# A man can climb.

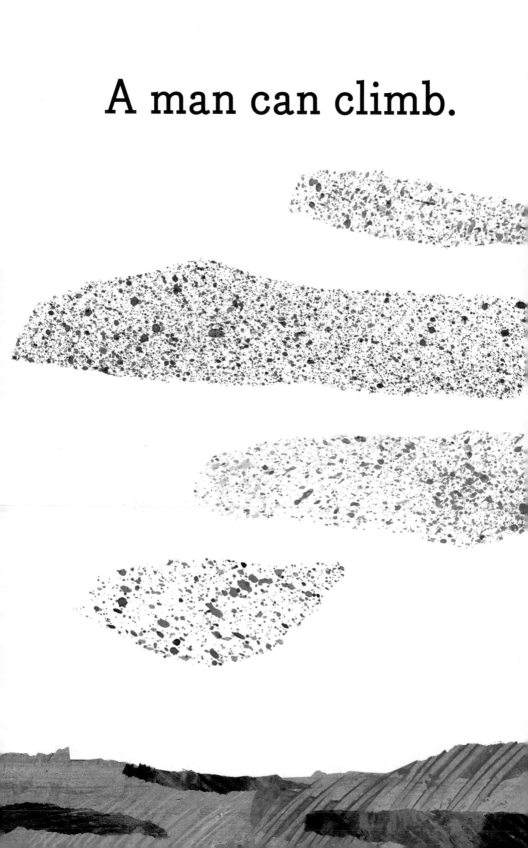

# Can a cat do that?

Yes!

A cat can climb.

# A girl can read.

# Can a cat do that?

No!

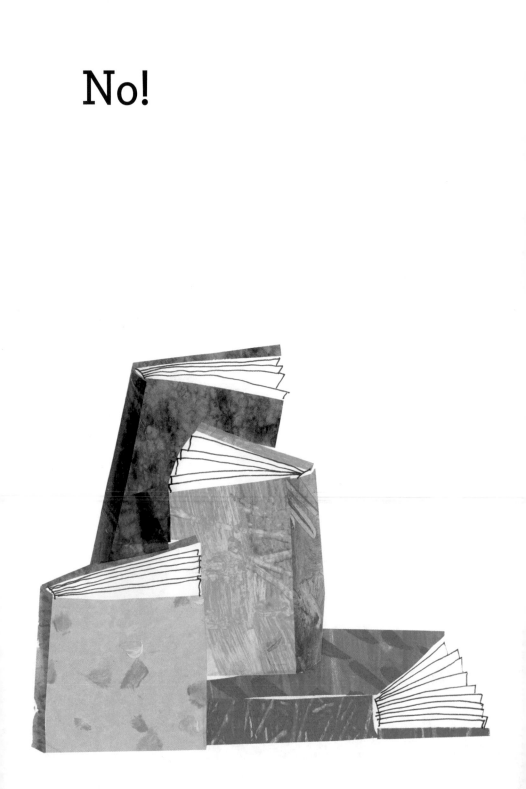

*Meow!*

I love my cat!
My cat loves me!

# Meow!

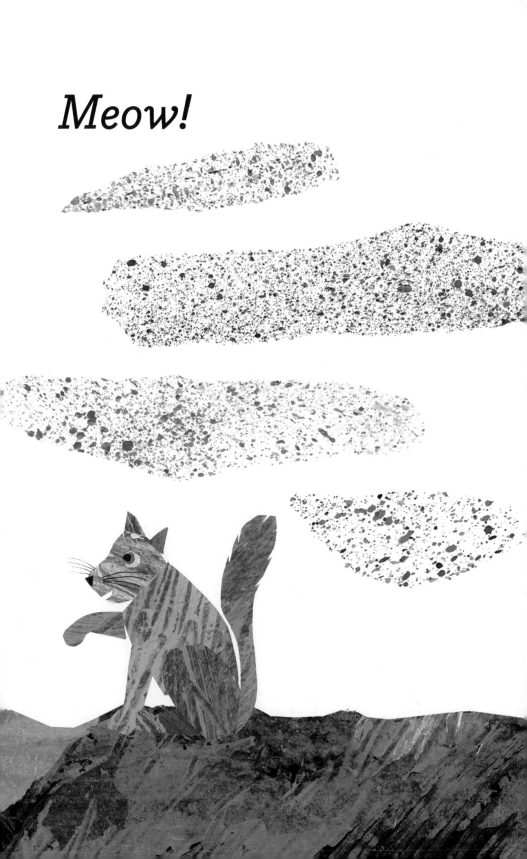

Now that you have read the story, you might like to try and answer these questions.

1. As you go back through the story, can you count how many things a cat can do? And how many things a cat cannot do?

2. There are many animals in this book. Which one is your favorite?

3. In this story, there are words that rhyme, such as "cat" and "that." Can you think of other words that rhyme with "cat" and "that"?

**Great job!**
**You are a reading star!**